ANNA AT THE ART MUSEUM

ANNA AT THE ART MUSEUM

HAZEL HUTCHINS & GAIL HERBERT * ILLUSTRATED BY LIL CRUMP

ANNICK PRESS
TORONTO · BERKELEY

Anna was not happy.

Everything at the art gallery seemed old and boring.

Anna would have to entertain herself.

"ROAR!" she said to the lion.
"Quiet please," said the attendant.

"Peekaboo," she whispered to the baby.
"Careful!" said the attendant.

When Anna carefully lifted her foot onto something that looked like it was for children, the attendant shook his head, no, and pointed to the sign.

So, Anna and her mother had a talk. It was one they'd had earlier, but perhaps Anna had not listened quite as closely as she should have.

No shouting.

No running.

No climbing.

No touching.

After that, Anna pretended she was
a small bush in a forest of tall trees.

One of the trees swayed to the side. There was something interesting beyond. Anna moved closer and closer . . .

Bing
Bing
Bing
Bing

Anna didn't know paintings could have alarms!

Everyone turned and stared. Anna quickly ran away.

On the second floor, Anna found
a window nook. While her mother looked
at paintings, Anna gazed longingly out at the street
and the harbor beyond.

If only the museum could be turned inside out.
Or the world outside in.

In the next gallery, she pulled out her snack.
But why was the attendant looking at her that way?

"Are you hungry?" she asked. "We can share."

He was not hungry. "No eating," he said with a firm voice.
She could only drink at the water fountain in the hall.

And then she saw the half-open door.

When a door is half open, it is very hard not to wonder what lies on the other side.

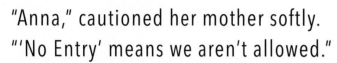

"Anna," cautioned her mother softly.
"'No Entry' means we aren't allowed."

"But . . ." Anna began.

Once again, the attendant was walking toward her. This time, however, he surprised her.

"It's not busy today. They might let you in. Would you like me to ask?"

It was like a secret workshop.

Here, art was studied, repaired, and cleaned.

As years of grime were removed, the face of a young
girl slowly emerged. It was a bored face, a grumpy face.

Anna knew that young girl.

She hurried to thank the attendant.

"She's just like me," Anna told him. "Or I'm just like her."

Which made the attendant smile.

And now, something had changed. On the floor
above, Anna danced patterns of her own.
She felt color swirl around her.

But it had been a long afternoon.
Even her mother was ready to go home.

They took the fast way down . . .

pausing only long enough for Anna
to whisper to the lion, "I'll be back."

Then they pushed open the wide gallery doors
and Anna skipped through, letting inside
and out flow together.

ABOUT THE ART

Anna's art museum is filled with a wide range of art by artists from many different eras and countries. Some of the pieces Anna sees are famous and some are lesser-known. Here is some information about the artworks and the people who created them:

HEAD OF A WOMAN,
circa 1650–1700, by Anonymous. French.
Black chalk on grey paper.
Metropolitan Museum of Art, New York.

o o o o o o o o o o o o o o o o

NUBIAN TRIBUTE PRESENTED TO THE KING,
TOMB OF HUY, circa 1353-1327 BCE.
Egyptian. Tempera facsimile by
Charles K. Wilkinson, circa 1923-27.
Metropolitan Museum of Art, New York.

o o o o o o o o o o o o o o o o

NEBAMUN SUPERVISING ESTATE ACTIVITIES,
TOMB OF NEBAMUN, circa 1400-1352 BCE.
Egyptian. Tempera fascimile by
Charles K. Wilkinson, circa 1928.
Metropolitan Museum of Art, New York.

o o o o o o o o o o o o o o o o

PANEL WITH STRIDING LION, circa
604-562 BCE. Babylonian from Mesopotamia
(Modern Hillah). Glazed ceramic.
Metropolitan Museum of Art, New York.

THE THIRD ICHIKAWA YAOZŌ AS A DAIMYO
STANDING UNDER A MAPLE TREE,
circa 1783, by Katsukawa Shunshō.
Japanese. Woodblock print on paper.
Metropolitan Museum of Art, New York.

o o o o o o o o o o o o o o o o

THE FIRST NAKAMURA NAKAZO AS A
SAMURAI STANDING NEAR A
WILLOW TREE, 1768 or 1769,
by Katsukawa Shunshō. Japanese.
Woodblock print on paper.
Metropolitan Museum of Art, New York.

o o o o o o o o o o o o o o o o

KABUKI ACTOR ICHIKAWA DANJŪRŌ V,
1774, by Katsukawa Shunshō. Japanese.
Woodblock print on paper.
Metropolitan Museum of Art, New York.

o o o o o o o o o o o o o o o o

MOTHER AND CHILDREN AT THE NEW YEAR,
18th century, by Utagawa Toyoharu.
Japanese. Ink and color on silk.
Metropolitan Museum of Art, New York.

ADOLESCENCE, OR SISTERS,
1976, by Daphne Odjig. Canadian.
Acrylic on Canvas.
Private collection.

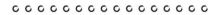

BROKEN EGGS,
1756, by Jean-Baptiste Greuze.
French. Oil on canvas.
Metropolitan Museum of Art, New York.

THE FOREST AT PONTAUBERT,
1881, by Georges Seurat. French.
Oil on canvas.
Metropolitan Museum of Art, New York.

WESTERN FOREST,
circa 1931, by Emily Carr.
Canadian. Oil on canvas.
Art Gallery of Ontario, Toronto.

THE SUPPER AT EMMAUS, 1601,
by Michelangelo Merisi da Caravaggio.
Italian. Oil and tempera on canvas.
National Gallery, London.

DER SCHREI DER NATUR (THE SCREAM),
circa 1893, by Edvard Munch. Norwegian.
Tempera and crayon on cardboard.
National Museum, Oslo.

REGATTA AT SAINTE-ADRESSE,
1867, by Claude Monet.
French. Oil on canvas.
Metropolitan Museum of Art, New York.

BRIDGE OVER A POND OF WATER LILIES,
1899, by Claude Monet. French. Oil on canvas.
Metropolitan Museum of Art, New York.

APPROACH TO VENICE,
1844, by J.M.W. Turner.
British. Oil on canvas.
National Gallery of Art, Washington, DC.

NATURALEZA MUERTA / STILL LIFE, 1908,
by Diego Rivera. Mexican. Oil on canvas.
Government of the State of Veracruz,
Xalapa, Mexico.

○ ○ ○ ○ ○ ○ ○ ○ ○ ○ ○ ○ ○ ○ ○ ○

STILL LIFE WITH ONIONS, JUG AND FRUIT,
circa 1930-38, by William H. Johnson.
American. Oil on burlap.
Smithsonian American Art Museum,
Washington, DC.

○ ○ ○ ○ ○ ○ ○ ○ ○ ○ ○ ○ ○ ○ ○ ○

THE PEPPERMINT BOTTLE,
1893/95, by Paul Cézanne.
French. Oil on canvas.
National Gallery of Art, Washington, DC.

○ ○ ○ ○ ○ ○ ○ ○ ○ ○ ○ ○ ○ ○ ○ ○

LITTLE GIRL IN A BLUE ARMCHAIR, 1878,
by Mary Cassatt. American. Oil on canvas.
National Gallery of Art, Washington, DC.

○ ○ ○ ○ ○ ○ ○ ○ ○ ○ ○ ○ ○ ○ ○ ○

GIRL IN A GREEN DRESS,
1930, by William H. Johnson.
American. Oil on canvas.
Smithsonian American Art Museum,
Washington, DC.

○ ○ ○ ○ ○ ○ ○ ○ ○ ○ ○ ○ ○ ○ ○ ○

PORTRAIT OF A YOUNG WOMAN,
late 18th century, unknown artist. Pastel.
Saint Louis Art Museum, Saint Louis.

WATER-MOON AVALOKITESHVARA,
first half of 14th century, unidentified
artist. Korean. Hanging scroll,
ink and color on silk.
Metropolitan Museum of Art, New York.

○ ○ ○ ○ ○ ○ ○ ○ ○ ○ ○ ○ ○ ○ ○ ○

THE SINGER IN GREEN,
circa 1884, by Edgar Degas.
French. Pastel on paper.
Metropolitan Museum of Art, New York.

○ ○ ○ ○ ○ ○ ○ ○ ○ ○ ○ ○ ○ ○ ○ ○

A WOMAN SEATED BESIDE A VASE OF
FLOWERS, 1865, by Edgar Degas.
French. Oil on canvas.
Metropolitan Museum of Art, New York.

○ ○ ○ ○ ○ ○ ○ ○ ○ ○ ○ ○ ○ ○ ○ ○

DANCERS, PINK AND GREEN,
circa 1890, by Edgar Degas.
French. Oil on canvas.
Metropolitan Museum of Art, New York.

○ ○ ○ ○ ○ ○ ○ ○ ○ ○ ○ ○ ○ ○ ○ ○

TWO DANCERS AT REST OR, DANCERS
IN BLUE, circa 1898, by Edgar Degas.
French. Pastel on paper.
Musée d'Orsay, Paris.

○ ○ ○ ○ ○ ○ ○ ○ ○ ○ ○ ○ ○ ○ ○ ○

UNDER THE WAVE OFF KANAGAWA OR, THE
GREAT WAVE, circa 1830-32, by Katsushika
Hokusai. Japanese. Woodblock print.
Metropolitan Museum of Art, New York.

For Theo and Isaac, with love. –H.H.

For Benjamin, who is always an inspiration. –G.H.

"You use a glass mirror to see your face; you use works of art to see your soul." –George Bernard Shaw
For Rachael, my favorite always, and for Bruce, my rock. Special mention to Ceilidh, the furry yellow dog that made my studio so warm and inviting. –L.C.

Designed by Antonia Banyard and Alexandra Niit
Cover designed by Alexandra Niit

Annick Press Ltd.

We acknowledge the support of the Canada Council for the Arts and the Ontario Arts Council, and the participation of the Government of Canada/la participation du gouvernement du Canada for our publishing activities.

Funded by the Government of Canada   Financé par le gouvernement du Canada

    ONTARIO ARTS COUNCIL
CONSEIL DES ARTS DE L'ONTARIO
an Ontario government agency
un organisme du gouvernement de l'Ontario

IMAGE CREDITS
Pages 30 to 33 constitute an extension of these credits and this copyright page.

All gallery art is public domain (Creative Commons Zero license) and can be found at the Metropolitan Museum of Art, with the following exceptions: Adolescence, or Sisters, by Daphne Odjig. © Odjig Arts. Used with permission; Western Forest, by Emily Carr, Art Gallery of Ontario, Toronto, Canada / Bridgeman Images; The Supper at Emmaus, by Michelangelo Merisi da Caravaggio, National Gallery, London, UK / Bridgeman Images; Der Schrei der Natur / The Scream, by Edvard Munch, World History Archive / Alamy Stock Photo; Approach to Venice, by JMW Turner, public domain, Courtesy National Gallery of Art, Washington, DC; Still Life with Onions, Jug and Fruit, by William H. Johnson, Smithsonian American Art Museum, Washington, DC / Art Resource, NY; Naturaleza Muerta / Still Life, 1908, by Diego Rivera, (scan) © Schalkwijk / Art Resource, NY, (artwork) © (2018) Banco de México Diego Rivera Frida Kahlo Museums Trust, Mexico, D.F. / SODRAC; The Peppermint Bottle, by Paul Cézanne, public domain, Courtesy National Gallery of Art, Washington, DC; Little Girl in a Blue Armchair, by Mary Cassatt, public domain, Courtesy National Gallery of Art, Washington, DC; Girl in a Green Dress, by William H. Johnson, Smithsonian American Art Museum, Washington, DC / Art Resource, NY; Two Dancers at Rest or, Dancers in Blue, by Edgar Degas, Musée d'Orsay, Paris, France / Bridgeman Images; Picture frames (various, throughout) © gillmar / Shutterstock.com, and © 501room / Shutterstock.com, and © stevemart / Shutterstock.com, and © Wittayayut / iStockphoto.com.

Cataloging in Publication

Hutchins, H. J. (Hazel J.), author
    Anna at the art museum / Hazel Hutchins, Gail Herbert ; illustrated by Lil Crump.

Issued in print and electronic formats.
ISBN 978-1-77321-043-8 (hardcover).--ISBN 978-1-77321-042-1 (softcover).--ISBN 978-1-77321-045-2 (ePUB).--ISBN 978-1-77321-044-5 (PDF)

    I. Herbert, Gail, author II. Crump, Lil, illustrator III. Title.

PS8565.U826A83 2018   jC813'.54   C2018-901610-8
                                        C2018-901611-6

Published in the U.S.A. by Annick Press (U.S.) Ltd.
Distributed in Canada by University of Toronto Press.
Distributed in the U.S.A. by Publishers Group West.

Printed in China.
www.annickpress.com
Find Hazel Hutchins at www.hazelhutchins.net
Find Lil Crump at www.ideahousedesign.com

Also available as an e-book. Please visit www.annickpress.com/ebooks.html for more details.